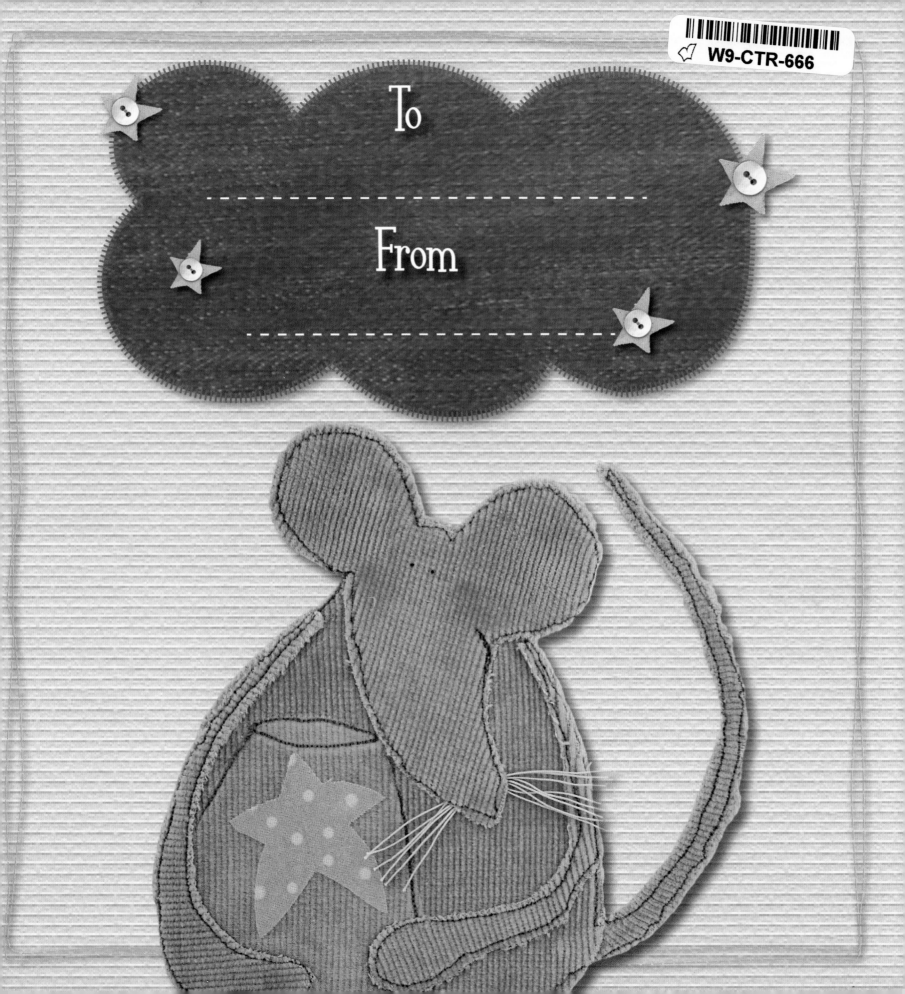

To

From

With thanks to Jane Horne.

Copyright © 2007

make believe ideas

27 Castle Street, Berkhamsted,
Hertfordshire, HP4 2DW.

Manufactured in China

TWINKLE TWINKLE LITTLE STAR

KATE TOMS

make believe ideas

Twinkle, twinkle,

little star,

How I wonder

what you are,

You **shine** above
the **world** so high,
Like a **lightbulb**
in the **sky**.

I'd love to catch you in my **net**...

and keep you as a special pet!

Twinkle, twinkle, little star,
I do so wonder what you are.

When snuggled up in bed at night,
Cozy, warm, and tucked up tight,

I dream that I can fly a rocket...

5 4 3 2

and gather stardust in my pocket.

And if the **moon** is made of **cheese**,

Yummy!

Will you save some for me, please?

Twinkle, twinkle, little star,

What do you see from afar?

Hello

Hola!

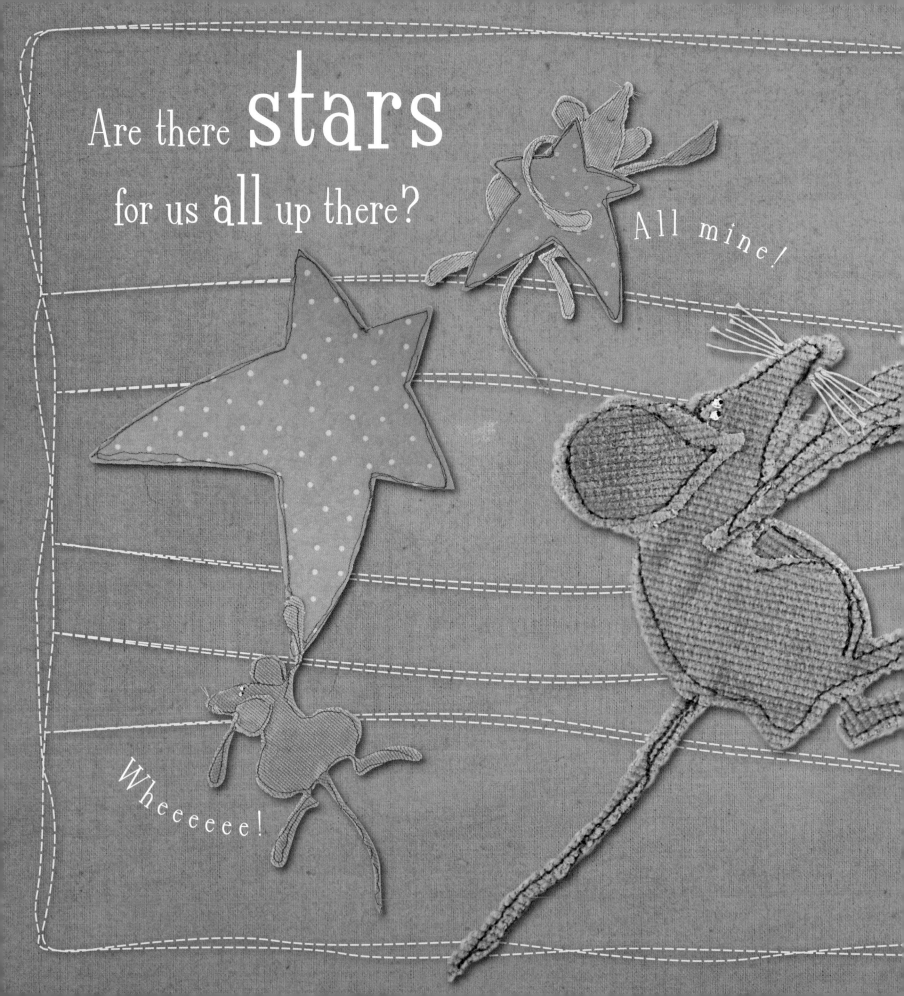

Are there **stars** for us **all** up there?

All mine!

Wheeeeee!

Jump!

Or do some folks have to share?

That you would look down
on my house,
And grant one thing
for this small mouse.

And see the world the way you do.

Twinkle, twinkle, little star,
How I wonder what you are.

When it's time to climb the stairs,

To **brush** my **teeth**
and say my **prayers**,

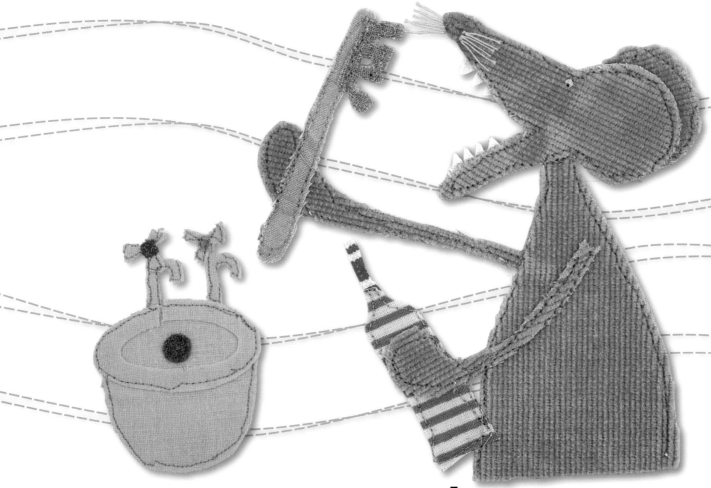

Through my **window** I can see,
That you are **smiling** down on me.

Twinkle, twinkle, little **star**, How I wonder what **you** are,